It Started As an

It started as an egg.
It hatched and it grew.

Its feathers grew so it could fly.
It started as an egg and it became an eagle.

3

It started as an egg.
It hatched and it grew.

4

Its hard shell grew to keep it safe.
It started as an egg and it became a turtle.

It started as an egg.
It hatched and it grew.

Its scales grew bright green so it could hide.
It started as an egg and it became a snake.

It started as an egg.
It hatched and it grew.

Its teeth grew strong so it could eat.
It started as an egg and it became a crocodile.

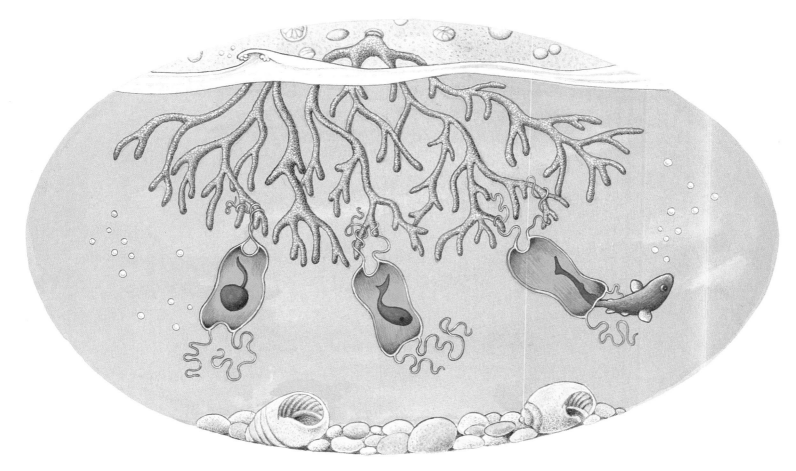

It started as an egg.
It hatched and it grew.

Its fins grew big so it could swim.
It started as an egg and it became a shark.

It started as an egg.
It hatched and it grew.

It grew legs so it could hop.
It started as an egg and it became a frog.

All of these eggs may hatch and grow.

What will they become?

ostrich

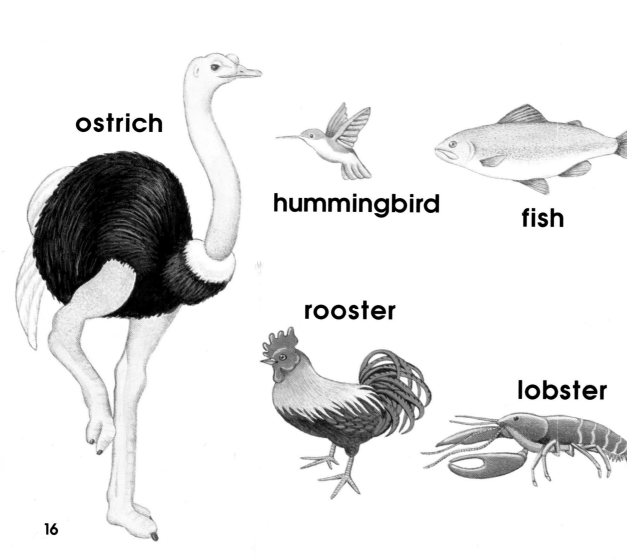

hummingbird

fish

ladybu

rooster

lobster

spider

ant